J
398.2    Freedman, Florence B. (Florence Bern-
F            stein)
             Brothers : a Hebrew legend / retold
         by Florence B. Freedman ; with illus-
         trations by Robert Andrew Parker. --
         1st ed. -- New York : Harper & Row,
         c1985.
             unp. : ill.                     slj K-2
             ISBN 0-06-021872-X (lib. bdg.) : 9.89
             SUMMARY: Hard times on adjoining
         farms bring about parallel acts of
         kindness and a celebration of "how good
         it is for brothers to live together in
         friendship."
             1.Folklore--Israel. 2.Brothers--Fiction.
PZ8.1.F87Br 1985                    76341          Ja86
                                dc19        85-42616
          CATALOG CARD CORPORATION OF AMERICA©    AACR2    CIP MARC AC    19

# BROTHERS

# BROTHERS

## A HEBREW LEGEND

retold by *Florence B. Freedman*

with illustrations by *Robert Andrew Parker*

*Harper & Row, Publishers*

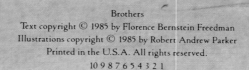

Library of Congress Cataloging in Publication Data
Freedman, Florence B. (Florence Bernstein)
    Brothers : a Hebrew legend.

    Summary: Hard times on adjoining farms bring about
parallel acts of kindness and a celebration of "how good
it is for brothers to live together in friendship."
    [1. Folklore—Israel.    2. Brothers—Fiction]
I. Parker, Robert Andrew, ill.    II. Title.
PZ8.1.F87Br   1985        398.2'1'095694 [E]        85-42616
ISBN 0-06-021871-1
ISBN 0-06-021872-X (lib. bdg.)

For my grandchildren—Miriam, Jenny,
John, Noah, Michael, and Lorin—and
for all grandchildren everywhere

—F.F.


For Harriett,
my mother

—R.A.P.

Long, long ago
in the land of Israel
lived a farmer named Seth.

Seth had two sons, Dan and Joel.

Every spring and every fall
Seth plowed the earth.
From the time they were little boys,
Dan and Joel followed him,
planting the seeds.

Then they watched the wheat grow
from tiny plants to tall stalks.

When the wheat grew tall,
Dan and Joel could hide in it.
It was taller than they were.

When the wheat was ripe,
Seth took his sickle
and cut it down.

The boys helped him
tie it in bundles
and load it onto their donkey.
Then they rode to the threshing floor
and piled the wheat high.

Dan and Joel grew and grew
until they were taller than the plow,
taller than the wheat...
taller than their father.

When Seth grew old,
he called his sons to him.

"You are good men and good farmers.
You are good sons to me and to your mother.

"I am too old
to plow and plant
and stack and thresh the wheat.
I will soon die.

"I will divide my land in half.
You, Dan, will get one part,
and you, Joel, the other.
I know that you will always be friends
and help each other."

After their father died,
Dan and Joel divided the land.
Each built a house.

Joel married a lovely woman
named Miriam.
Dan did not marry.
He lived alone.

Time passed.
Miriam and Joel had three sons.
Joel added rooms to his house.
His sons helped their father,
just as Dan and Joel
had helped their father.

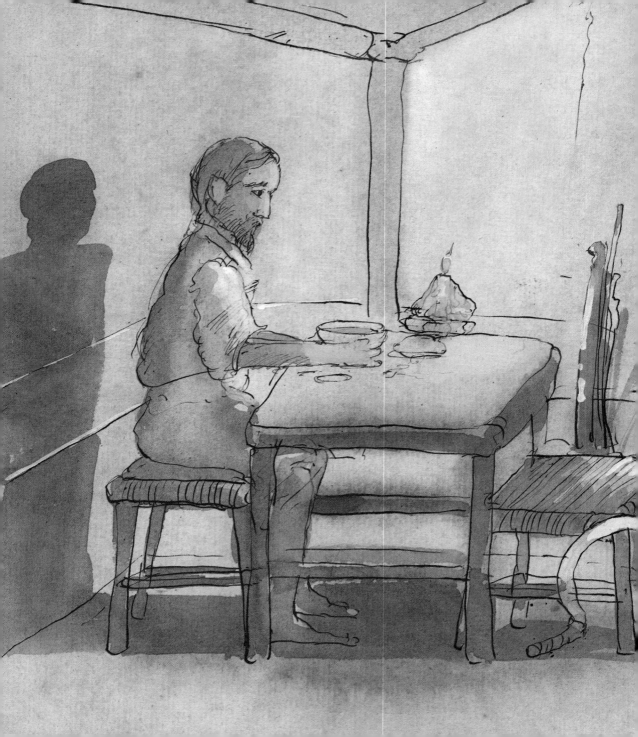

Dan did not marry.
He lived alone in his little house.
He went to visit Joel and his family
whenever he could.

When Joel's boys
were twelve and ten
and three years old,
there came a bad year.
The rains did not fall.

The wheat dried up.
There were not many
bundles of wheat
on the threshing floor.

One night Joel could not sleep.

"What is the matter?" asked Miriam.

"I am thinking about my brother.

He is all alone.

You and I have sons

to take care of us

when we are old.

Dan has nobody.

Yet we have the same amount of land

and the same amount of wheat.

It isn't fair."

"What will you do about it?" asked Miriam.

"I know," answered Joel.

"I will take some of my wheat

to my brother."

It was almost midnight.
Joel dressed quickly
and left the house.
He shook his sleepy donkey.
"Wake up! We have work to do!" he said.

In the quiet of the dark night
he took wheat to his brother's threshing floor
and silently went home.

On the same night
Dan could not sleep.
He was thinking about his brother.

"My brother Joel has a wife
and three children.
He has five people to feed
and I have only myself.
Yet he has the same amount of land.
It isn't fair," he thought.

Quietly he got out of bed,
loaded his donkey with wheat
and took it to his brother's threshing floor.

In the morning Joel looked at his wheat.

He rubbed his eyes.

"Can it be?

There is just as much wheat here today
as there was yesterday.

I must take more to Dan tonight."

In the morning Dan too looked at his wheat.
He rubbed his eyes.
"I did not take my brother
as much wheat as I meant to," he thought.

That night again
Joel took wheat to Dan,
and Dan took wheat to Joel.

In the morning
each had as much wheat
as he had had
the day before.

Joel told his family what had happened.
"Tonight we will help you,"
said Miriam and the boys.

That night Joel awakened
Miriam and the boys.
"It is time," he said.
They loaded the donkey,
and Joel, Miriam and the boys
carried as much wheat as they could.

That night Dan started out
with his load of wheat
at the same time as Joel.

They met halfway,
at the place where their farms joined.

Without saying a word,
they dropped their bundles of wheat
and hugged each other.

Then they heard a soft voice
that came from everywhere and nowhere
singing,
"How good it is for brothers
to live together in friendship."

Hundreds of years passed.
A city grew where Seth's farm had been—
the city of Jerusalem.
And King Solomon built the Holy Temple
on the spot
where the brothers had met
and hugged each other.

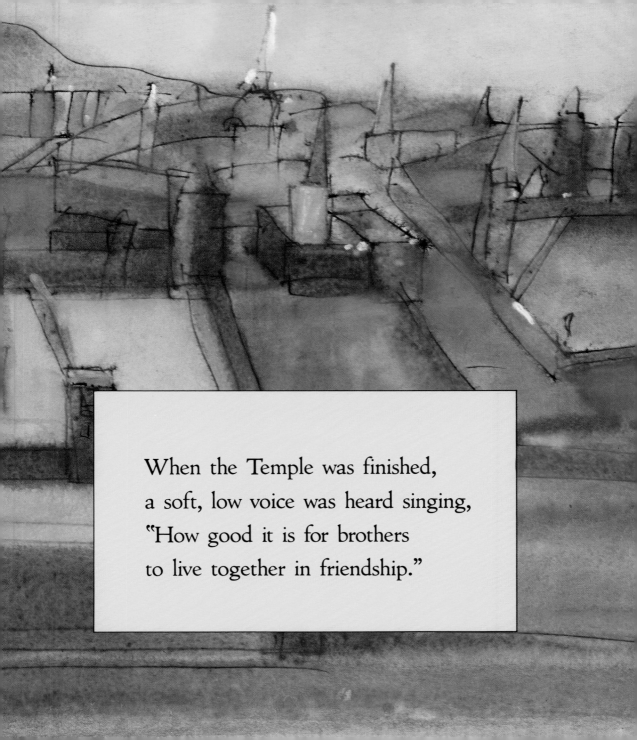

When the Temple was finished,
a soft, low voice was heard singing,
"How good it is for brothers
to live together in friendship."

The song came from nowhere—
and everywhere.